Out of the Nursery

1ˢᵗ Edition

Frog Legs Ink is an imprint of Gauthier Publications.
www.GauthierPublications.com

All illustrations in this book were done on scratch paper. Cover art done in watercolor and ink on illustration board.

Proudly printed and bound in the USA

Library of Congress Control Number: 2008907832

ISBN 13: 978-0-9820812-0-4

Out of the Nursery

Written and Illustrated by Elizabeth Gauthier

Frog Legs Ink

To Genevieve

Long live story time!!

Tick tock ... tick tock,
What's wrong with the clock?
I saw the mouse run inside,
From the cat he tried to hide.
He went in at precisely one,
Just as the chiming had begun.
Now the ringing just won't stop.
I think the mouse is stuck up top.
Tick tock ... tick tock,
Can't someone fix the clock?

Starlight you're just too bright.
You're the only thing I see at night.
I wish I may, that you just might
Let me get some sleep tonight.

No one knew why she picked that shoe.
The rooms were certainly small.
Once she only had three kids,
Now she couldn't count them all.
She put on a new addition,
Taking the shoe from a size five to a ten.
No matter what arrangement she tried,
She couldn't fit them all in.
She got up one day, had had enough.
This arrangement would no longer suit.
She grabbed all her kids, packed up their clothes,
And moved to a spacious boot.

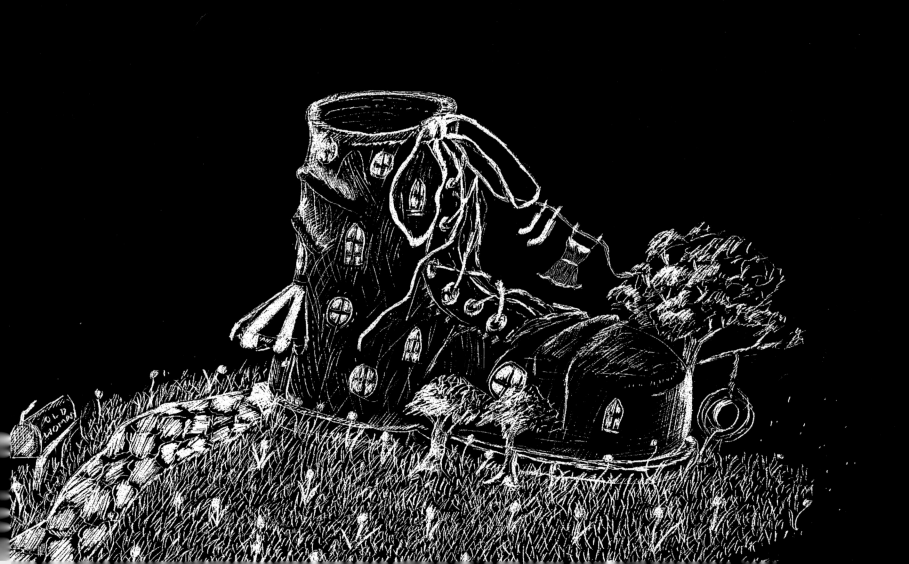

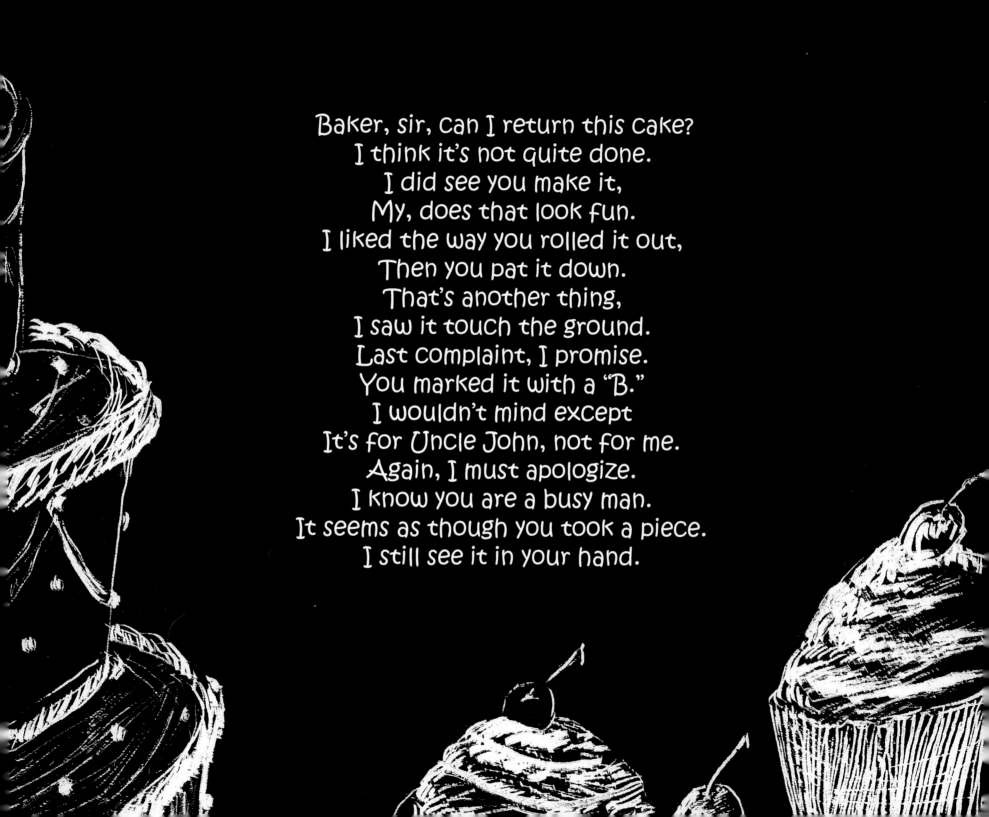

Baker, sir, can I return this cake?
I think it's not quite done.
I did see you make it,
My, does that look fun.
I liked the way you rolled it out,
Then you pat it down.
That's another thing,
I saw it touch the ground.
Last complaint, I promise.
You marked it with a "B."
I wouldn't mind except
It's for Uncle John, not for me.
Again, I must apologize.
I know you are a busy man.
It seems as though you took a piece.
I still see it in your hand.

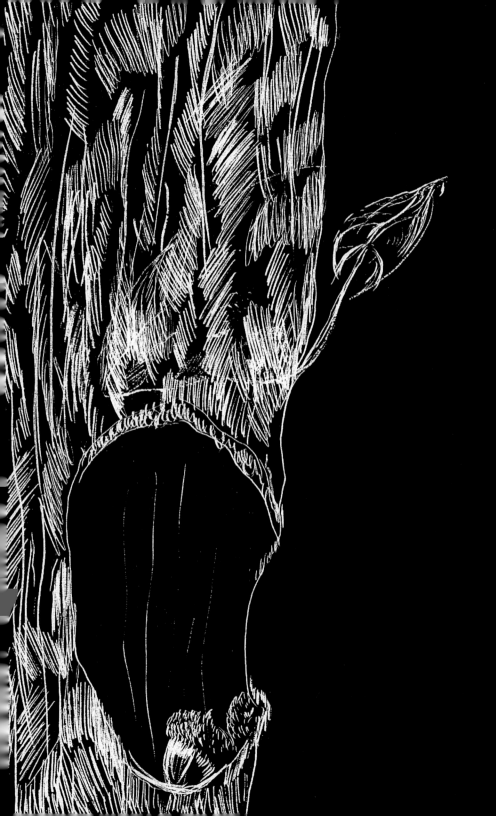

Peep, she lost her sheep.
She has been crying for a day.
We all have our theory,
Agreeing he wouldn't run away.
We put him on milk cartons,
Missing signs were drawn,
A search party formed,
Passing them out to everyone.
Two weeks now and sheep returns.
He must have missed his life.
Of course Peep wasn't mad,
He came home with a wife.

The hill was steep,
Almost straight up.
The bucket didn't help.
One wrong step,
And he tumbled and rolled,
As dear Jill let out a yelp.
Now they are in bed
With their get well cards,
Happy to do no work or chore.
Best of all knowing,
They wouldn't be asked
To climb that steep hill anymore.

There she sat,
Calm as can be,
Eating her curds and whey.

Relaxing and resting,
She was tired
From hours of games and play.

When suddenly
A giant spider
Came and ruined her day.

He crept on by,
Sat down and
Looked as though he'd stay.

Arachnophobia,
She suffers now,
Is what her doctors say.

Now poor little girl
No longer sits to eat her
Curds and whey.

The cat played the fiddle
Almost every night.
But cow couldn't stand it,
It gave him such a fright.

So he decided it'd be better
To live up on the moon.
Knowing the cat,
He'd better make it soon.

He plotted with the dog,
Who thought it just a riot,
Never once considering
Cow would actually try it.

It was a failure.
He really overshot.
Now dog is convincing him
The sun is much too hot.

In the end, I'm not sure why
The dish up and ran.
Now the spoon is leaving,
That I understand.

Row, Row, Row,
A one track mind they had.
The stream was gentle enough,
It was the singing that was bad.

Twenty times they went around
Singing the nautical tune.
On and on they went,
With no signs of stopping soon.

One hundred times he listened,
He couldn't tell what was worse –
Jumping out to swim
Or listening to the repetitive verse.

Walking out onto the beach,
His clothes were sopping wet.
A small price to pay
To escape the lyrics he'd like to forget.

I scrubbed for hours,
All the king's men with me.
We were all in need of showers
After moving the yellow debris.

When all was said and done,
I couldn't get so mad.
Though it wasn't very fun,
He was the best breakfast I ever had.

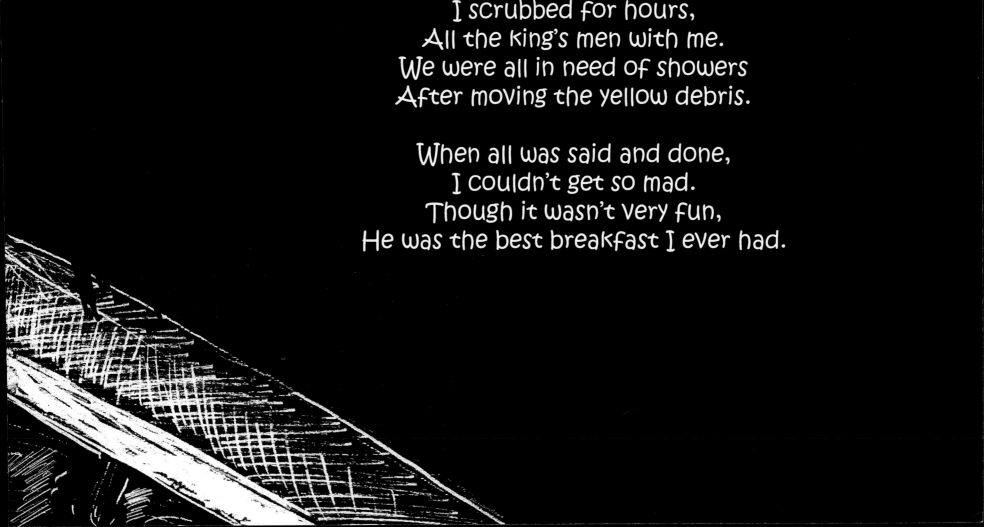

Big
Jump
Today

He may have jumped the candlestick,
But his ego grew too large.
He wasn't ready just yet
To take on the sizable barge.

People came from everywhere,
It was a spectacle from the start.
He showed up in costume,
He was really into his part.

He waved to the crowd, started to run,
And began the impossible jump.
Thankfully landing bottom first,
His head was saved a lump.

Spider wasn't big,
He was an itsy bitsy guy.
But he still climbed that waterspout
That reached up to the sky.

It was frustrating to say the least,
The weather kept changing its mind.
Every time the sun came out,
The rain wasn't far behind.

An hour straight, he continued up,
He could almost see the light.
Three times the charm, he thought,
As the clouds came into sight.

Faster and faster he went,
But it all went down the drain.
Just as spider touched the top,
It began to rain.

He was so very proud,
His black coat always full.
He'd shave it off immediately,
Giving out all his wool.

Bags and bags he passed out
To the young and to the old.
But now that generous little sheep
Is always very cold.

Free
Wool

The

End